DAISY SAVES THE DAY

For Alice with love

❧

First U.S. edition 2015

Library of Congress Catalog Card Number 2013955680
ISBN 978-0-7636-7323-9

14 15 16 17 18 19 SCP 10 9 8 7 6 5 4 3 2 1

Printed in Humen, Dongguan, China

This book was typeset in Filosofia.
The illustrations were done in ink, gouache, and watercolor.

Candlewick Press
99 Dover Street
Somerville, Massachusetts 02144

visit us at www.candlewick.com

DAISY SAVES THE DAY

Shirley Hughes

CANDLEWICK PRESS

ONCE, NOT SO VERY LONG AGO,
there was a girl named Daisy Dobbs. She had a
Mum and two little twin brothers, and they
were very hard-up.

At school the teacher said that Daisy was
exceptionally bright. She could read and do
beautiful handwriting and solve figures in
her head.

But often, when Mum was out at work, Daisy
had to stay at home and look after the twins.
She longed to have some books of her own
to read, but they were too poor to buy any.
Instead, she made up wonderful stories and
told them to the twins at bedtime.

Then the sad day came when Mum told
Daisy that it was time for her to leave school
altogether and go out to work too.

"I've got you a job as a scullery maid," she said. "It's in a very nice home owned by two ladies, the Misses Simms, very refined. There's a cook and a parlor maid, so the work won't be too hard. And you'll be living in, get your keep and all."

"You mean I won't be living at home with you and Tommy and Billy anymore?" asked Daisy sadly.

"No, but you'll have your own uniform, a half-day off every week, and one whole Sunday a month."

So one spring morning, very early, Mum left the twins with a neighbor, and she and Daisy set out from their home on the far outskirts of London, carrying all Daisy's belongings in a small suitcase.

It was a very long journey into the city, first by train and then a weary walk from the station. At last they arrived at the house where the Misses Simms lived. It was a tall house in a row of other tall houses, with lace curtains in every window except for the attic.

They went down the basement steps to the back door and rang the bell.

The parlor maid answered. "So, you're the new scullery maid," she said, looking Daisy up and down. "Bit young for the job, aren't you?"

"She's a very good worker," said Mum anxiously.

"You'd better start right away then. There's plenty to do, I can tell you."

Daisy was very sad to say good-bye to Mum. But she bravely managed not to cry.

Soon she was wearing a cap and a big apron over her blue cotton dress and was set to work washing dishes, scouring saucepans, and peeling potatoes for the cook.

Miss Jessie and Miss Margaret Simms were quite old. They sat in the front parlor by a big coal fire. When they wanted something, they rang the bell for the parlor maid, whose name was Ellen. She did a lot of running up and down the stairs, which made her cross. But not as cross as Cook, who toiled endlessly over the big hot kitchen range, preparing meals and baking scones and cakes.

Daisy was not very good at housework, but she worked very hard. She swept the stairs and carried buckets of coal for the fires and helped with the laundry. She scrubbed the front doorstep and polished the knocker till it shone.

"This looks very nice, Daisy," said Miss Jessie encouragingly as she and Miss Margaret were setting out for their morning walk.

"Thank you, ma'am," Daisy replied, remembering to curtsey.

At the end of each day she was very tired. After supper Ellen and Cook sat chatting by the kitchen fire. Daisy knew that they wanted to have a grown-up gossip, so she did not try to join them. Instead she went up to her little attic bedroom and huddled under her blanket, missing Mum and the twins and longing for her day off. Even when that came she could not afford the fare home.

But now summer was on the way, and there was great excitement in the quiet house. The Misses Simms' niece, Miss Mabel Simms, was coming for a visit all the way from America.

On the day of her arrival they were all in the hall to greet her. She was tall and untidy and wore her hat on the back of her head.

"I sure am glad to meet you all!" she said, and shook hands with all the servants, even Daisy.

She was a very friendly lady.

One day when Daisy was bringing in the coal for the parlor fire, Miss Mabel asked if she could read.

"Oh, yes, Miss." She looked longingly at the bookcase. "When I was at school it was my favorite thing in all the world."

"Me too. I'll ask my aunts if you can borrow one of these from time to time."

After this Daisy did not feel so lonely. Some of the books were too difficult for her to read, but others had pictures and they were her favorites. She took them up to her room and pored over them whenever she could. She especially loved stories about princesses, kings, and queens.

That summer was a very special one because the new king, George V, was going to be crowned. Miss Mabel had timed her visit especially to see the coronation procession. Daisy went out into the streets whenever she could to see the Union Jack flags flying everywhere and red, white, and blue streamers wound around the lampposts.

Miss Jessie and Miss Margaret Simms, though they were very patriotic, considered all this a little vulgar. Their house was the only one on the street that remained undecorated. Daisy thought that was a sad shame.

GOD SAVE THE KING

When the great day came, the three ladies set out very early. They had been invited to watch the procession by some friends whose house overlooked the route.

Cook and Ellen had the day off and were going out too. But Daisy was to be left all alone. They told her that she was too young to go out among all the crowds and that she was to stay indoors all day.

After they had gone, Daisy
wandered slowly upstairs to her
room. From her little attic window
she could see the people celebrating
in the street below, and she could
just hear the brass band playing
in the park. It all seemed like a
wonderful storybook adventure,
and she wanted to be part of it.
She watched for a long time.

Then she had a good idea. She went
downstairs and found the spare clothesline
and some clothespins. She picked
out some white pillowcases and blue
dishcloths, but she needed something red.
The only red things Daisy could find were the
scarlet flannel bloomers that the older
Misses Simms wore in cold weather.

Daisy took them upstairs to her room
and pinned them firmly on the line,
alternating red, white, and blue.

Then she tied one end of the line to her window latch and let the other drop. It hung right down in front of the house, fluttering festively in the breeze.

Passers-by laughed and pointed when they saw it. They looked up and waved at Daisy, and she waved back. She felt she was part of the celebrations at last.

But when the Misses Simms came home that evening and saw their red bloomers hanging out for all to see, they were gravely displeased. Daisy would have been dismissed on the spot and sent home in disgrace—if it had not been for Miss Mabel.

She thought the whole thing was a huge joke and managed to persuade her aunts to give Daisy another chance.

"She is only young, and she wanted to join in," Miss Mabel said.

After this, Daisy was kept in disgrace. Ellen and Cook hardly spoke to her except to order her around, and they gave her all the nasty chores to do. When her day's work was done, she was too tired even to read.

One Sunday the three ladies went out
visiting. Ellen had the evening off,
and Cook was settled in her chair
in front of the kitchen fire.

Daisy went miserably up to
her room.

It was chilly up there.
She curled up under her blanket,
shed a few tears, and went to sleep.

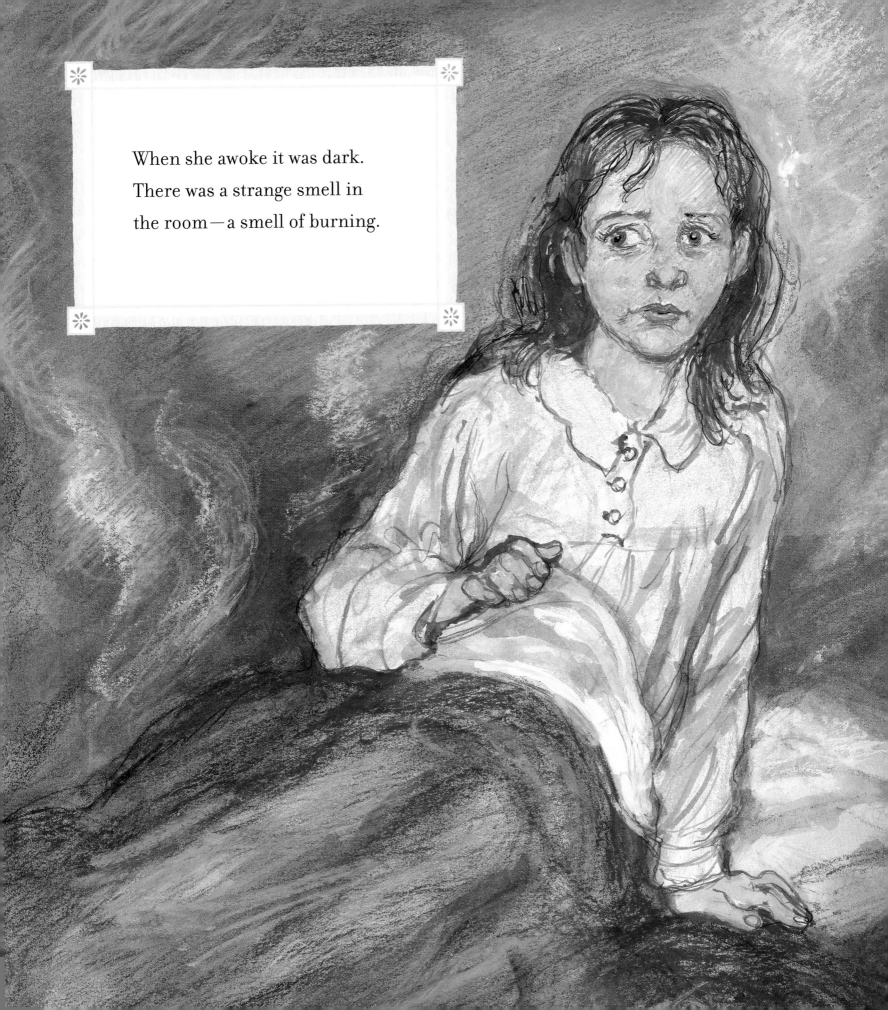

When she awoke it was dark.
There was a strange smell in
the room—a smell of burning.

Daisy scrambled up, flung open her
bedroom door, and ran downstairs.
The hall was full of smoke. When
she reached the kitchen there was Cook,
slumped fast asleep in her chair, and
the dishcloths that she had hung near the
kitchen range to dry had caught fire.
They were already ablaze.

Daisy shook Cook awake, and together they ran to fill jugs and saucepans with water from the kitchen sink. They sloshed it over the flames. There was a horrible sound and the smoke made them cough, but they had caught the fire just in time.

Daisy had saved the day.

"Thank heavens you discovered it when you did," said Miss Jessie when the ladies returned.

"You are a brave girl, Daisy," said Miss Margaret.

"You can say that again!" said Miss Mabel.

The next morning Daisy was summoned to the parlor, where all three ladies were assembled.

"We've been discussing how to reward you for your prompt and plucky action," Miss Jessie told her. "Without it, this house would have been badly damaged, perhaps even with loss of life. So my niece, Miss Mabel, has come up with this suggestion which I hope will be acceptable to you. As you don't seem very well suited to domestic work—"

"I've tried my best, Miss," said Daisy anxiously.

"Of course, we know that. But it seems to me that you are better at reading than at polishing and scrubbing. And we thought that as a reward your mother might see fit to accept a sum of money from us to pay for your schooling."

"You mean I could go home, Miss?"

"Yes," said Miss Mabel. "You will be able to attend school again regularly, and if you do well you might go to the grammar school next year."

"So I won't be in service anymore?" asked Daisy with a gasp.

"Just that, Daisy," said Miss Mabel, smiling broadly. "If you agree, that is!"

For a moment Daisy was speechless. She was thinking about going home to Mum and the twins, and being able to learn and read again, and tell stories to them.

Her nose turned bright pink.

"Oh, yes please, Miss!" she said at last.

THE END